WIND RIDERS

SEARCH FOR THE SCARLET MACAWS

RIDERS

SEARCH FOR THE SCARLET MACAWS

WRITTEN BY JEN MARLIN

ILLUSTRATED BY IZZY BURTON

HARPER

An Imprint of HarperCollinsPublishers

ISBN 978-0-06-302929-3 (paperback)—ISBN 978-0-06-302930-9 (hardcover)

Typography by Joe Merkel

21 22 23 24 25 PC/LSCC 10 9 8 7 6 5 4 3 2 1
❖

First Edition

For Shelley, in memory of our rain forest adventure

With special thanks to Erin Falligant

CONTENTS

CHAPTER 1

ANOTHER ADVENTURE

"Uh-oh, a waterfall!" cried Max.

He held his breath as the toy boat lunged forward, caught in the rushing water of the rocky stream. For a moment, the tiny wooden vessel hung suspended—half in the water, half out. Then it plunged, nose first, over the edge.

"Yes!" cried Sofia. "That was our best run yet." She leaned over the stream and collected the model boat from a mass of leaves and twigs.

Cold raindrops trickled down the back of her neck, and she squealed. "This rain just won't let up!" She gazed past the marina toward the sandy beach, where the air was thick like a misty gray curtain. She and her parents were visiting Starry Bay for the summer, and this was their first day without sunshine.

3

Max laughed. "Grandpa knew it was coming, because he saw a halo around the sun when we were out on his boat this morning." As a retired fisher, Max's grandpa knew everything there was to know about the weather, the sea, and boats. He'd even helped them carve the wooden boat that they were playing with.

The model was fun, but Max couldn't stop thinking about a boat he and Sofia had sailed together for real. His gaze drifted to the mangrove forest behind them.

Sofia caught his eye. "Are you thinking

4

what I'm thinking?" she asked.

"*Wind Rider*?" Max whispered, as if someone might overhear.

"Exactly."

Just a few days ago, the old sailboat they had found in the mangrove forest had magically transformed into a brand-new boat and taken them on an amazing adventure in Hawaii.

"Did we really sail across the ocean?" Max asked. The whole thing felt like a dream.

Sofia grinned. "We really did. I just hope we'll get to do it again one day." They had tried boarding the boat yesterday and spinning the creaky wooden helm. But this time, nothing had happened.

"You never know," said Max. "I guess we'll just have to wait and see."

Sofia sighed. "I was never very good at waiting." She handed Max the tiny wooden boat.

Max was about to take it, when something landed on the rock beside him.

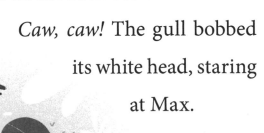

Caw, caw! The gull bobbed its white head, staring at Max.

Max sucked in his breath. He *knew* this bird, with its long yellow beak and smooth gray feathers. It was the seagull that had first led them to *Wind Rider*!

The bird cocked its head and gave another caw. Then it half flew, half hopped toward the mangrove forest.

Sofia gasped. "It wants us to follow!" she cried. "Maybe it's time for another adventure!"

She raced after the gull, with Max in hot pursuit.

As Max ducked under hanging moss,

his heart raced. Sofia had disappeared in the tangle of branches and leaves ahead. "Wait for me!" Max called, leaping over a thick root.

When he reached the clearing, he saw that Sofia was already on the deck of the weathered old boat. *Wind Rider* tilted sideways, half in the water and half out. Warped boards bulged from its navy-blue hull.

"Come on!" Sofia cried over the rail. Her stomach fluttered like the tattered sail overhead. She knew that no time would pass while they traveled on *Wind Rider*. They'd be back before anyone at home missed them.

The seagull swooped low beside her, as if it were anxious to get started, too.

"Where are we going this time?" Sofia asked the bird, wishing she could speak its language. The last time they had sailed on *Wind Rider*, they had helped some baby sea turtles.

Max climbed up the squeaky metal ladder and over the rail and landed on the slippery deck with a *thud*. He headed straight toward the wooden helm at the stern of the boat, where Sofia joined him.

"Ready?" she said.

Together, they reached out toward the wheel and gave it a mighty spin. A cold breeze began to blow. The helm started to spin, faster and faster by itself, and the sail above unfurled and flapped to life.

"Hang on!" cried Max, grinning from ear to ear. Sofia closed her eyes against a blur of blues and greens. Her hair

whipped wildly around her head.

Then the wind died down. The boat bobbed gently.

When Sofia opened her eyes, she saw that they weren't on ocean waves.

Wind Rider, now freshly painted, sailed lazily down a wide brown river. Dense thickets of lush green trees lined either side. Vines snaked up the tall, skinny tree trunks, and the branches spread over them into a thick canopy.

"Where are we?" Sofia asked.

A trickle of sweat ran down Max's

forehead. "It's really hot," he said, wiping his face with his T-shirt.

"And what's that sound?" Sofia asked, cocking her head. "Birds?" She checked for the seagull that had led them to the boat, but it was gone. *Just like last time*, she remembered.

Max held his breath, listening to the low chorus of hums, chirps, and buzzes that rose from the forest.

"It sounds like birds and insects," he said. "Millions of them!"

Sofia craned her neck, hoping to see

some animals. But the canopy of trees was too thick. The air felt thick, too—so different from the breezy shore of Starry Bay. "It feels like it could rain at any minute," she said. "Or like it just did." She ran her hand along the damp rail of the boat.

Max snapped his fingers. "That's it!" he cried. "*Rain.* It's a rain forest, Sofia."

Her eyes widened. "And this river is so wide, it must be . . ."

"The Amazon!" Max and Sofia said at the exact same time. "We're in the Amazon rain forest!"

CHAPTER 2

PAULO

"Ooh, I hope we're right about this being the Amazon," said Sofia. "My mom says *millions* of animal species live here."

She leaned over the rail toward the densely wooded riverbank, scanning the tall, skinny trees and the vines and bushes for signs of animal life.

Max tugged on the back of her shirt. "I know you love animals," he said with a grin. "But don't fall in!"

"I can't see anything from here anyway," Sofia sighed.

"Let's go below deck," Max suggested. "There might be some stuff down there that can help us figure out what we're here to do."

They hurried over to the wooden hatch, which led to a metal ladder. Rung by rung, they climbed down to the cabin, which was illuminated by sunlight streaming through the portholes. They raced past the small kitchenette and stopped beside a long, low bookshelf.

A giant atlas lay on a table, just as it had on their last adventure. As Max and Sofia came closer, the book flipped open, and its pages turned quickly in a blur and finally settled down.

"We *are* in the Amazon rain forest," Sofia declared, pointing at the page. "In Brazil. See?"

Max studied the map, which showed a wide river winding through a patch of green. "Yes! We were right!" He offered Sofia a fist bump. "But wait . . . I don't know very much about Brazil. Do you?"

"Not really," Sofia confessed. "Hey, let's see if there's anything in here!" She walked to the big sea chest carved with animals. "Remember, last time the chest had snorkeling gear, which was just what we needed for our adventure."

The top of the chest was made of heavy wood, but Sofia was able to get it open without much trouble. "Look!" At the bottom of the chest lay two beaded necklaces alongside a pair of flashlights and bug spray. Sofia picked up one of the necklaces and saw that the beads were different shades of brown, as if each had been made from a different type of wood.

"What do we do with those beads?" Max asked.

Sofia was already putting on her necklace. "We wear them," she said, as if he'd asked the silliest question in the world.

Max shrugged and put his on, too. "I guess we'll also need these," he said, grabbing one of the flashlights.

Sofia nodded and reached for the other one, and motioned to the can of bug spray.

"Don't forget this. We don't want to get eaten alive by mosquitoes."

"Good idea!" Max said as he sprayed himself all over.

As Max followed Sofia back up to the

deck, he noticed that the trees were much closer now—and much taller. "I think the boat is taking us ashore!" he said.

They waited, full of excitement, as they drifted closer to the riverbank. Tree branches reached out over the water, beckoning them forward. Then *Wind Rider* lurched to a stop.

"Is there a dock?" Max asked, glancing down at the murky water. The sandy riverbank was still several yards away.

"Who needs a dock?" said Sofia.

When Max turned around, he saw Sofia

reaching toward the branches of the tree that hung over the deck.

She heaved herself up onto a branch, and the wooden beads dangled from her neck. "Come on!" she said to Max, grinning.

Max followed, carefully crawling along the tree limb, pushing past its shiny, rubbery leaves. When he reached the thick trunk, Sofia was already climbing down, using a tangle of vines as a ladder.

As her feet hit the rain forest floor, Sofia breathed in deeply. Down here, below the canopy of trees, the world felt dark and shady. She glanced around, searching for a path through the tangled tree roots, rocks, and leaves. "Which way now?" she asked.

Max dropped to the ground beside her. "I don't know," he said. "Just keep your eyes open for anyone—or anything—that might need our help."

As he and Sofia passed by the vines and waxy plants, they could hear a faint pitter-patter of water dripping from leaves all around. Birds called to each other, so different from the *caw, caw* of the seagull that had brought them here. Max looked overhead, hoping to see the gull, but he couldn't even see the sky—the trees were so thick!

They eventually found a narrow path and walked for what felt like hours, until the trees began to spread out and shafts of sunlight lit the ground.

Max hoped to see a town up ahead. What he saw instead stopped him in his tracks. The barren ground was littered with burnt tree stumps. The lush green forest had given way to ashes.

"What happened?" Sofia cried. "Was there a fire?"

"Exactly," someone answered. But it wasn't Max.

Sofia whirled around and noticed a boy about her age picking his way across the dark ground. He wore a bright yellow shirt and a sunny smile, which instantly put Sofia at ease.

"Are you lost?" the boy asked as he got closer. "Are you tourists?"

Max cleared his throat. "Yes—I mean, no. Um, sort of."

The boy nodded. "We used to get a lot of tourists," he said. "Not so much anymore." He held out his hand. "I'm Paulo."

Max and Sofia introduced themselves, too. "What happened here?" Max waved his hand across the burned-out field.

Paulo's face fell. "A rancher set a fire to clear the land for farming," he explained.

"That's what my cousin Antonio told me. But it was so dry and windy, the fire got out of control. It destroyed all this forest and drove a lot of animals away from their homes."

"What kinds of animals?" asked Sofia, frowning.

Paulo sighed. "Sloths, jaguars, and monkeys. And birds—toucans and my favorite, the scarlet macaws. We had huge flocks of scarlet macaws." He searched the sky, as if hoping a macaw might fly overhead at any second.

"But now?" He shrugged. "I know of only one tree with a macaw nest in it. I'm on my way there, because the eggs will hatch any day. I need to be sure the chicks are safe."

"Can we come with you?" The words flew out of Sofia's mouth.

She and Max glanced at each other hopefully.

This sounds like an adventure, Max thought.

Paulo's face spread into a smile. "Of course!" he said. "Follow me!"

CHAPTER 3

TRUST THE MAGIC

As Paulo led the way back into the lush green forest, Max could once again hear the pitter-patter of water drops and the chirping of birds and insects.

Paulo seemed to know exactly where he was going. He pushed past palms and stepped over the tangled roots easily. Sofia and Max followed closely behind.

"Is the nest far?" asked Max.

"No," Paulo said. He gave them an approving smile. "For tourists, you both speak very good Portuguese."

"Huh?" Sofia's jaw dropped open.

"Um, thanks," said Max. But as soon as Paulo was out of earshot, Max grabbed Sofia's hand. "I thought Paulo was speaking English!" he whispered.

"Me too!" said Sofia. "Turns out we're speaking his language."

Max's eyes drifted down to the wooden beads around her neck. "I think I understand," he said. He reached for his own necklace and slipped it off over his head. Then he waited.

"*Como vai?*" Paulo called from the trail ahead.

Como what? Max cocked his head, then put the beaded necklace back on. "What was that, Paulo?" he asked.

"I asked how it was going back there," said Paulo—in perfect English.

Max grinned. "That's what the necklaces are for!" he whispered to Sofia. "They help us speak Paulo's language!"

"I *told* you to trust the magic," she whispered back with a smile.

"So what do you know about scarlet macaws?" Paulo asked when they caught up to him.

"I know they're parrots," said Sofia.

"That's right," said Paulo. "Large parrots with red, yellow, and blue feathers. They can live up to forty or fifty years in the wild, at least if their home is protected. They eat fruit, nuts, and seeds. Insects, too, and the nectar of flowers. Oh, and they also eat dirt and clay."

"Huh?" asked Max. "That sounds, um . . . tasty." He wrinkled his nose.

Paulo laughed. "I don't know if it tastes good, but I think the clay gives them minerals they need—that's what Antonio says, anyway. They get it from walls of clay, where the water has eroded the riverbank. We call them clay licks. You should see how many macaws can gather at one clay lick at a time. It's amazing!"

"I hope we do," said Sofia, crossing her fingers.

Finally, Paulo stopped beside a palm tree. "This is it," he whispered. The tree looked dead, with only a few brown leaves sprouting from the top of its tall, skinny trunk.

"Where's the nest?" asked Sofia, glancing up.

Paulo pointed toward a hole in the trunk, high above the ground. "The nest is built in the knothole. C'mon, let's climb this rubber tree for a closer look."

Paulo started up a nearby tree that had glossy, oval-shaped leaves. He used the vines that were wrapped around the thick trunk to pull himself up.

Sofia scrambled up behind him, eager to see the nest. As Paulo scooted out onto a branch, she followed. "Here," he said, holding out the binoculars.

She held them to her eyes. At first, all

she could see was
the gray trunk of
the tree. But as she
slid the binoculars
downward, the knot-
hole came into view.
And just inside? She
saw two little chicks,
with bald gray heads
and tiny beaks.

Sofia gasped. "They hatched! The chicks hatched!" She reached out a hand to steady herself and handed Paulo the binoculars.

As Max slid onto the branch beside Sofia, a patch of red caught his eye. A macaw swooped down from the branches above and landed on the edge of the knot-hole of the palm tree. "Look," he breathed, nudging Sofia.

Paulo lowered the binoculars. "The parents are here," he whispered. He pointed toward a second macaw resting at the top of the palm. "They've brought food for the chicks."

The adult macaws' brilliant red heads and brightly colored wings stood out like tropical flowers against a field of green, and their long tail feathers stretched regally toward the ground. *They must be almost three feet long!* Sofia marveled.

With a sudden screech and a flutter of wings, one of the parents swooped past the tree where Sofia, Max, and Paulo were perched.

Squawk!

Sofia's heart raced as she clung to the branch to stop herself from falling. "Why did it do that?" she whispered.

"We're too close to the nest," said Paulo. "Let's climb back down to show them we're not a threat."

As Max made his way back down to the ground, he felt uneven grooves in the bark. "Hey, look," he said, once they reached the ground. "Someone carved something into the tree."

Paulo's brow furrowed. "Oh no. That means someone else knows about the chicks. And this"—he touched the carving that was shaped like an *X*—"means they're planning to cut this tree down."

"But why?" asked Sofia. Her cheeks flushed hot. "Who would cut down a tree with chicks in it?"

Paulo gave a sad sigh. "It's the easiest way to steal the chicks! Some people sell them as pets at the market. It's why lots of macaw species are endangered. And cutting down the tree is doubly bad, because then macaws can't use it as a nesting place in the future."

"That's awful!" cried Sofia.

As Paulo crouched down to look more closely at the footprints, Max grabbed

Sofia's arm. "I think this is why *Wind Rider* brought us here," he said in a low voice. "To help the macaw chicks and save their nest."

Sofia nodded. "I think you're right."

Max threw an arm around Paulo's shoulder.

"Don't worry," he said. "We won't let anyone hurt the chicks."

"We're going to help you protect them," added Sofia, her eyes flashing.

But they were both thinking the same thing . . .

How?

CHAPTER 4

UNDER THE ELEPHANT EARS

"Whoever is planning to steal the chicks will be back soon," said Paulo in a tight voice. "Probably when it gets dark."

"Then we'll spend the night here," said Sofia. She planted herself in front of the tree, her arms crossed. "We won't let anyone take them."

Paulo shook his head. "It's too danger-ous to wait in plain sight. We don't know who's coming . . . or what they'll do to get those chicks."

"Then we'll hide!" said Max. "If some-one comes, we can jump out to stop them. And if they look dangerous, we can run for help. There are *plenty* of places to hide around here, like . . . under one of these plants with those huge leaves." He reached out to stroke a waxy, heart-shaped leaf that was nearly as long as he was tall.

"The elephant ear plant?" asked Paulo with a smile.

"Hey, those leaves *do* look like elephant ears!" said Sofia, studying the plant. "Is there room for all three of us?"

Max dropped to his knees to test it out. "Definitely," he decided. As moisture seeped through his shorts, he hurried back out. "But we might want to bring something to sit on."

Paulo looked curious. "Are you two sure you can spend the night guarding the nest with me? I'm sure my mom won't mind.

I camp out in the forest all the time. But what about you? Won't your families wonder where you are?"

"Our folks won't miss us," Sofia promised.

Max raised an eyebrow at her, and she gave him a small shrug.

I'm not lying, she reasoned to herself.

"Okay, great," said Paulo. "We have a few hours before night falls. I'll take you to my mother's restaurant in town, not far from here. You can meet her and Antonio. And we can pick up some food there."

Instead of leading them back the way

they'd come, Paulo seemed to head deeper into the rain forest. He picked up his pace, pushing through the trees so quickly that Max and Sofia had to race to keep up.

After a while, the trees began to thin out. Max's heart quickened when he spotted a small town up ahead. Wooden houses

and buildings lined a single street. In a field nearby, a group of kids played soccer beside a large community garden.

As Sofia followed Paulo down the street, she noticed a group of people spilling off a boat onto a small pier. "Are those tourists?" she asked. Some had sunburned noses

beneath their straw hats. Others wore binoculars around their necks.

Paulo nodded. "I'm happy to see so many of them," he said. "My mother will be, too."

But Max noticed that the tourists didn't seem quite as happy. They looked, well . . . *bored.* "What a disappointment!" one woman said. "So much of the forest just burned down."

"I know," said another, shaking her head. "It's so sad. . . . And hardly any animals to be seen."

Sofia glanced at Max. "Paulo did say

that lots of animals were driven away from the forest," she whispered. "Like the flock of scarlet macaws. Where do you think they went?"

Max shrugged sadly. "I don't know. But this is bad. We have to make sure we keep those chicks safe."

"Here we are," called Paulo, waving them toward a small, run-down building near the water. A faded sign reading *Juliana's* was nailed above the door.

Inside, the tables were nearly empty. Photographs of the rain forest hung on yellow walls whose paint was peeling, and the sweet scent of fried dough wafted from the back of the restaurant, making Max's mouth water.

"Paulo!" called a woman who stepped from the back room. She swiped a strand of dark hair back into her bun and smiled warmly.

"Hi, Mom," Paulo said, giving her a quick hug. "These are my friends Max and Sofia. They're visiting."

"Welcome!" said the woman. "You can call me Juliana. Are you hungry? We've got

lots of space." As she waved her arm around the restaurant, her face fell. "We used to be much busier, but since the fire, well . . . there are so few tourists." Her eyes flicked back to Paulo and she forced a smile. "Have you come for some black bean stew?"

"No, thanks," he said. "We're hoping to pick up some food to go. For . . ." He faltered.

"For a picnic dinner!" Sofia quickly added. She glanced at two men sitting in the corner. Were they listening in? She wasn't sure, but if Paulo was keeping the macaw chicks a secret, she would, too.

Juliana nodded. "You speak very good Portuguese," she said to Sofia.

Sofia flushed. "Thank you," she said. She stroked her wooden beads and shot Max a quick smile.

Juliana wiped her hands on her striped apron. She cupped her hand and called into the back room. "Antonio!"

A young man with a mop of curly hair appeared in the doorway. When he saw Paulo, he grinned. "Hey, cousin!" He threw an arm around Paulo and ruffled his hair.

"Stop that!" Paulo laughed and ducked

out from under Antonio's arm.

"You know, I remember when he was just a little baby," Antonio teased. "So cute!"

Paulo rolled his eyes. "Aren't you supposed to be working?"

"Always," said Antonio. "Hey, did I hear you were having a picnic? I've got some fresh *pastéis*, coming right up." He disappeared back into the kitchen.

"Antonio and I are always exploring the rain forest together," said Paulo. "And he fishes, and helps my mom out here, too."

"What are *pastéis*?" asked Max.

"Crispy dough filled with vegetables," said Paulo, licking his lips. "Mom makes the best *pastéis* in town. Hopefully Antonio didn't ruin them." He pointedly glanced at his cousin, who had reappeared with a brown bag.

"Hey, I heard that!" Antonio shot back. "Not nice." He held the bag high, just out of Paulo's reach.

"C'mon, now," said Juliana, hurrying them toward the door. "Don't disturb the customers. And don't be back too late tonight, Paulo, all right?"

Paulo nodded, but Max saw a shadow cross his face.

Who knows what—or who—we'll find

in the forest tonight? Max thought with a shiver. *Whoever is after the macaw chicks, we're going to catch them.*

And it wasn't just the chicks in danger. If the birds didn't return to the rain forest, it looked like Paulo's mom's business would be ruined, too.

Chapter 5
A DARK FiGURE

"Ouch! That was my foot," gasped Max. He nudged Sofia sideways.

"Did I step on it? Sorry!" she whispered. "There's not very much room under here." As she shuffled away, water dripped from the elephant ear leaves above her head.

"What was that?" asked Max. He shook his collar and felt something trickle down his back. "Are there ants in here?"

Paulo stifled a giggle. "Don't worry, they're harmless," he said. "Some animals in the rain forest are dangerous, but they mostly steer clear of people. We'll hear more birds and frogs now that it's getting darker. Listen." He put his finger to his lips.

As if on cue, a bird sounded above the buzz of the cicadas. *Tonk, tonk, tonk!*

"That sounded like a bell ringing," said Max.

Paulo nodded. "It's called a bellbird."

Something roared overhead, and Sofia froze. "What was that? A lion?"

Paulo laughed. "There are no lions in the Amazon. That was a howler monkey," he said.

The cry echoed through the treetops, followed by a few grunts. Then a low growl.

Even Paulo whirled around this time, his eyes wide. "I don't know what that was," he whispered.

Max burst out laughing and pointed at

Sofia. "I do," he said. "It was Sofia's stomach."

"Sorry!" said Sofia sheepishly. "I think it's time for the *pastéis*."

When Paulo handed her the fried treat, she dove right in. Warm vegetables oozed out from the crispy crust. "Yum," she said, instantly taking another bite. "Your family can really cook!"

Paulo sighed. "My mom's recipes are great. I only wish there were more people visiting so they could appreciate them."

Sofia nodded. "It would be terrible if she had to close her restaurant."

"Shh!" Max whispered. He'd just heard something—the crunch of leaves and twigs. He held his breath, listening.

Snap! Crack!

Sofia gasped. She gripped Max's arm and pointed.

Through the leaves of the elephant ear plant, they saw a dark figure step into view. A tall, thin man slid a bag off his shoulder and set it on the ground. He unzipped the bag and pulled something out.

An axe! Max realized. *He's here to cut down the tree!*

Adrenaline shot through his veins. But before he could move, Sofia burst out of their hiding place. Blinding light filled the forest as she flicked on her flashlight. Paulo was right behind her. "Stop right there!" he shouted. The man flung his arms over his eyes to block the light.

Paulo gasped.

"Antonio?"

With a jolt of surprise, Max recognized Antonio's dark eyes and mop of curly hair.

As Sofia lowered her flashlight, Antonio blinked. "Paulo?" he asked in a wobbly voice. "Is that you?"

"What are you doing?" Paulo cried, his voice rising.

Antonio's shoulders slumped.

"Those chicks are worth so much money," he said, so quietly that it was almost a whisper.

Paulo kicked furiously at the dirt.

"I can't believe you would do that! How could you be so greedy?"

"It's not for me!" Antonio said quickly. "It's for your mom. So she doesn't have to close the restaurant." He hung his head. "I know it's wrong," he said. "But I didn't know what else to do. Things are bad, Paulo."

Paulo stared at his cousin, his face softening. Sofia felt her own anger drain from her.

Finally, Paulo spoke. "But there must be another way to save the restaurant that won't harm the macaws or the rain forest."

Antonio raised his eyes from the ground. He looked uncertain.

"We'll figure something out together," said Max. "Right, Sofia?"

"Right," she answered brightly.

But how?

As they began the long walk out of the dark forest, Sofia waved her flashlight back and forth, wishing the way forward was clear.

CHAPTER 6
FOLLOW THAT BIRD!

"What are we going to do?" Sofia asked Max. Her whole body felt weary, even though they had spent the night in comfortable beds at Paulo's house. They had told Juliana that their parents wouldn't mind them staying over. Which was true,

Max knew—because no time would have passed when they returned to Starry Bay.

Max sighed. Not even the bright yellow walls of Juliana's restaurant could cheer him up this morning. He shrugged. "What *can* we do?"

"We can eat," Paulo announced. He gestured toward Antonio, who was bringing out a plate of rolls. "Brazilian cheese bread. Best breakfast ever."

Antonio set the bread rolls on their table. He had dark circles under his eyes, as if he hadn't slept a wink. "Listen, I just wanted to say again . . . I'm sorry."

Paulo lowered his voice to a whisper. "I know," he said. "You were just trying to help."

Antonio gave a weak shrug. "If only there were more macaws around—flocks of them, like there used to be—the restaurant wouldn't be in trouble. The tourists loved the macaws!"

Sofia bit into a roll and wiped crumbs

from her chin. "Could we find them?" she asked. "Could we figure out where the flocks of macaws went after the fire?"

"I don't know," said Antonio. "I only know where the one nest is."

As Juliana called Antonio back into the kitchen, Max had a sudden thought. "Paulo, you said macaws like clay licks. Maybe we could find one."

Paulo looked up. "They're usually found in river bends," he said, "where there's lots of mud and sandy clay."

"We could follow the macaws," said

Sofia thoughtfully. "If the parents of the chicks fly to a clay lick during the day, they could lead us there!"

Max slapped his hand on the table so hard that his fork rattled. "That's it!"

Paulo didn't look so sure. "Following birds through the rain forest won't be easy. But . . . it might be the best chance we've got."

* * *

A short while later, Sofia, Max, and Paulo were hurrying through the rain forest toward the macaw nest. They struggled to keep their eyes on the sky without tripping on the undergrowth below.

Suddenly, Sofia saw a blur of red. Two scarlet macaws flew overhead. "There they are!" she cried, pointing.

"Let's go!" said Max.

Together, they led the way over dead branches and around bushes and vines. Max kept his eyes trained on the scarlet birds that flitted from tree to tree, until he tripped and sprawled in a heap of damp leaves.

"Are you all right?" Paulo asked, reaching down to help him.

Max nodded. "Thanks." But as he took a moment to catch his breath, he saw that Sofia had stopped running, too. "Where'd they go?" she asked, staring at the sky. As she spun in a slow circle, her heart sank. "Did we lose them?"

"No," said Paulo. "I can still hear them cawing in the distance."

Max studied the dense canopy of leaves. "Maybe we just need to get up a little higher." He reached for a vine wrapped around a tree trunk, tugging on it to see if it would hold him.

"Good idea," said Paulo. "Wait, take these." He handed Max the binoculars.

Max hung the binoculars around his

neck and began to climb, hanging on to the vine. When he reached the lower branches of the tree, he studied the sea of green around him, hoping to spot a speck of red.

He saw nothing.

So he climbed higher, until he found a gap in the leaves. Here, sunlight warmed his face. He felt as if he could see for miles.

He scanned the treetops, searching for the red wings of the macaws. As his eyes drifted past a patchwork of color, he paused. He pressed the binoculars to his eyes and searched until he saw it again—a

flash of reds, yellows, and blues, so bright it could have been a rainbow-colored towel on the beach in Starry Bay.

Max rubbed his eyes and adjusted the binoculars.

There! This time, he zoomed out until he could see the brilliant patch of color set against a muddy riverbank. His heart thudded in his ears.

"I see the clay lick!" he cried, nearly losing his balance. He peered again through the binoculars. "And there are tons of scarlet macaws there!"

Max heard a rustle of branches below, and Sofia's head popped out from the leaves. It sounded like Paulo was close behind.

"We found them?" she asked, reaching for the binoculars.

Max couldn't stop smiling. "We found them!"

CHAPTER 7

A SURPRISE FOR ANTONIO

"There he is!" Max cried.

It was afternoon now, and he and Sofia had been waiting by the pier near Juliana's. Now Max had spotted Paulo coming around the corner toward them, followed by a group of tourists.

Sofia studied their faces. They looked every bit as disappointed as the group she had seen yesterday. *But not for long,* she thought. *Our plan has to work!*

Sofia and Max waved to get the tourists' attention. "The tour isn't over yet!" called Max.

"Come with us to our final stop on the tour!" cried Paulo. "Satisfaction guaranteed!"

The tourists didn't seem convinced. But they followed Paulo to Antonio's fishing boat, which was tied to the other side of the dock. Antonio was already sitting on board, looking confused. "Want to tell me where we're going?" he called to Paulo.

Paulo gave him a nervous smile. "Not yet. We'll direct you."

If we can remember the way, thought Max.

Paulo spread out a few cushions on the deck of the boat. "Sit here, sit here!" he said, helping an elderly man onto the boat. As soon as the tourists were seated, he reached for the rope to cast off. Then Sofia and Max joined Antonio at the stern.

"Head downriver," said Max, pointing

ahead. "Follow the curve."

It was a beautiful day in the rain forest. The sun filtered through green leaves and glimmered on the water. Sofia would have found it relaxing if she hadn't been so nervous about their plan. Behind her, tourists were beginning to grumble. "Where are we

going?" she heard a woman ask. "This is the same as the last tour. No animals at all."

Sofia peeked out from behind the wheel and saw tourists shifting in their seats and starting to stand. Paulo met her gaze. He nibbled his fingernail anxiously and leaned forward, as if willing the boat to go faster.

As the boat rounded the bend, Sofia searched for the inlet that would lead them where they wanted to go.

Her heart leaped. "There it is!" she said, pointing.

Antonio frowned. But he steered the boat into the long, narrow stretch of river all the same.

Sofia crossed her fingers that they were leading Antonio and his boat full of tourists in the right direction.

She sucked in her breath as the clay lick slowly came into view.

Yes!

It was *covered* with scarlet macaws! They blanketed the muddy banks like patches of wildflowers in a barren desert. When one took off, two more would land. Others

circled and squawked overhead, waiting for their turn.

Max gasped. "They're everywhere!" he cried.

The tourists had begun to chatter excitedly, whipping out their phones to take pictures. As the brilliant red birds wheeled around the boat, there was a chorus of oohs and aahs.

"*This* is more like it," said one of the ladies who had been grumbling.

Amid the murmur of happy voices and screeching macaws, Max barely heard

Antonio step up beside him. "A clay lick," Antonio said in disbelief. "So close to town? But I thought the macaws were gone!"

"They may have moved their nests," said Max. "But they still come here to feed on the clay." He breathed a sigh of relief as he gazed at the colorful birds clustered on the reddish-brown clay.

Paulo crossed the boat in one joyful bound. "It's perfect, isn't it?" he said to Antonio. "You can take tourists here on your fishing boat. And once tourism picks up again, no one will need to cut down trees and sell macaw chicks. More tourists will mean more business for Mom's restaurant, and for all our neighbors, too!"

Antonio smiled. "It's a great plan, cousin." He laughed and ruffled Paulo's hair. "We'll have to be careful, though. More tourists will mean more litter and more pollution. We'll have to think about how to manage it."

Sofia grinned. Antonio was clearly determined to make up for what he'd been planning with the macaw chicks.

Max caught Sofia's eye. He pointed to

the macaws circling overhead and mouthed the words, "We did it!"

Squawk! The macaw that flew past seemed to be celebrating, too.

Sofia laughed out loud and then followed the bird with her gaze. She didn't want to miss a single moment.

CHAPTER 8

FEATHERS

The noisy hum of voices made Max feel as though he were back under the elephant ear plant, listening to cicadas. But he was in Juliana's restaurant, where happy tourists were chattering and laughing. At every table, people shared stories and photos of the scarlet macaws.

"I've never seen anything so beautiful," a woman was telling her husband. "We'll have to let our friends know about this."

A man at another table held up his phone. "I'm going to post a few photos online," he said. "What's the name of this place again?"

"Juliana's," Paulo piped up. As he swiveled back to face Max and Sofia, he whispered, "Business will really pick up now!"

His mother squeezed his shoulder. As she set down a plate of steaming *pastéis*, she smiled. "Maybe we should rename the restaurant," she said. "How about 'The Scarlet Macaw'?"

"Yes!" said Max. "You could paint the walls red, and the window frames yellow and blue."

"And hang photos of the macaws," added Sofia.

"That would be a great way to celebrate them," said Paulo. "But . . ." He frowned.

"What is it?" asked Sofia.

"I only wish there were a way to stop more fires from destroying their nesting spots," he said. "If we had more money, maybe we could protect this part of the forest from fire damage."

"Then we'll just have to *raise* more money," said Sofia. "Like a scarlet macaw fund or something."

She felt someone tap her arm. "Did you mention a scarlet macaw fund?" asked the woman behind her. "I'd like to donate to that, if I could."

Sofia blinked. "Of course!" she said. "Um . . ." She scanned the restaurant, searching for a jar, bag, or box—anything she could pass to collect money. *If the tourists want to help save the macaws, we should let them!* she thought.

Paulo quickly emptied the napkins, knives, and forks out of a jar on the table. "Here!" he said, offering it to the woman. "You can be the first to donate money to protect the scarlet macaws." He caught Sofia's eye and winked.

As the jar circled around the restaurant, it began to fill with bills and coins. "Maybe tourists will donate after every tour!" Max whispered to Paulo.

Caw, caw! A birdcall came from outside, as if saying, *Yes! Good idea!*

But as it sounded again, the hair stood up on the back of Max's neck. "That wasn't a macaw," he said to Sofia. "That was a *seagull.*"

Her eyebrows shot up. She crossed the room to the window, where she could see *Wind Rider* slowly gliding up alongside the dock. The navy hull and white sail looked so fresh and new against the weathered boards of the pier. Sofia felt a sudden pang of homesickness.

"Is it time to go?" Max asked as she sat back down.

She nodded. "I think so."

"Go where?" asked Paulo.

"Home," said Max. "Our boat just arrived." He started to get up, then hesitated. It was so hard to say goodbye to new friends!

Paulo's face fell, but as the jar made its way back to him, he brightened back up. "Thank you for helping me save the scarlet macaws," he said, lifting the jar filled with money. "The baby chicks are in their nest, the forest will regrow, and one day, maybe all the macaws will return to our forest."

Sofia and Max said their goodbyes and slowly walked down the dock toward *Wind Rider*. Paulo and Juliana followed them out. A moment later, Antonio came, too. "Wait!" he called. "I have something for you. I found these on the deck of my boat."

He pulled three long feathers from his apron pocket. Sofia marveled at the brilliant red base and the bright blue tip. She could almost imagine the macaw that had shed it while flying high above the clay lick.

"Thank you," said Max as he gently reached for a feather.

"No, thank *you*," said Juliana, with a warm smile. "Thank you both for all you

have done for the macaws, and for
our restaurant."

Antonio handed the last feather
to Paulo. As Sofia and Max climbed up
onto *Wind Rider*, Paulo waved his feather
in the air. "Goodbye!" he called as the boat
pulled away from the dock.

Max waved, too, until the boat rounded the bend.

The sails flapped overhead as the breeze began to pick up.

"Let's get these feathers somewhere safe before they blow away!" Sofia called to him.

Belowdecks, they placed their feathers on the shelf beside the carved sea chest. There was a perfect spot for them, right next to the turtle eggshell they'd been given in Hawaii. They admired their growing collection for a few moments before *Wind Rider* began rocking in a most familiar way.

"We're going home!" Sofia cried, and she and Max scurried up to the deck.

Max hung on to the rail next to his friend as the boat picked up speed. As he squeezed his eyes shut, the wind roared around him. He heard the caw of the gull and then . . . silence.

When he opened his eyes, the sailboat was beached in the mangrove forest again, as if it had never left. *But Sofia and I know better*, he thought with a smile.

"C'mon!" called Sofia. They climbed down the ladder and raced through the forest. As she stepped out of the thick mass of trees, raindrops were still sprinkling down from the sky, and the stream gushing alongside the forest was swollen with rainwater.

Max hopped over the stream to join her. "Look!" he cried, pointing.

Through the rain, a rainbow could be seen stretching across the sky. The bands of red, green, and blue were especially vivid.

"It's beautiful!" said Sofia. "Almost as beautiful as . . ." She didn't finish her sentence, but she was thinking of the macaws.

"Almost," said Max, because of course, he'd been thinking the very same thing. He shot one more glance over his shoulder at the mangrove forest, picturing the sailboat hidden within. "Where will it take us next?" he wondered out loud.

A bird cawed overhead.

Sofia laughed. "That's seagull for, 'You'll just have to wait and see.'" Then she rubbed her stomach and added, "I know where I'm going next."

"Where?" Max asked.

"Dinner," she said with a grin. "Maybe

I can get my parents to look up a recipe for *pastéis*!"

Sofia knew her parents would do their best. But nothing would ever compare to Juliana's cooking. Maybe one day she and Max would get to travel back to the Amazon and try it again. After all, stranger things had happened.

THE *WIND RIDER* LOGBOOK

Sofia's sketch of *Wind Rider*

caBin

hELm

STeRn

hull

mast

SeaGull

Sail

porThole

bow

windRIDER

anchoR

OUR RAIN FOREST ADVENTURE

After taking us to Hawaii, *Wind Rider* brought us to the Amazon rain forest in Brazil. The Amazon rain forest is a huge area of warm, wet forest that stretches across eight countries in South America, and the Amazon River, which runs through it, is the largest in the world. The rain forest is full of animals. Sadly, many of them are endangered by deforestation. This is caused by people setting fires that spread through the forest, and by people cutting down trees to sell as timber or to build or create farmland. For example, Brazil is the world's largest exporter of beef, and ranchers need grazing land for their cattle, so they cut down acres of trees.

As well as destroying animals' habitats, deforestation is also damaging to the environment in all kinds of ways.

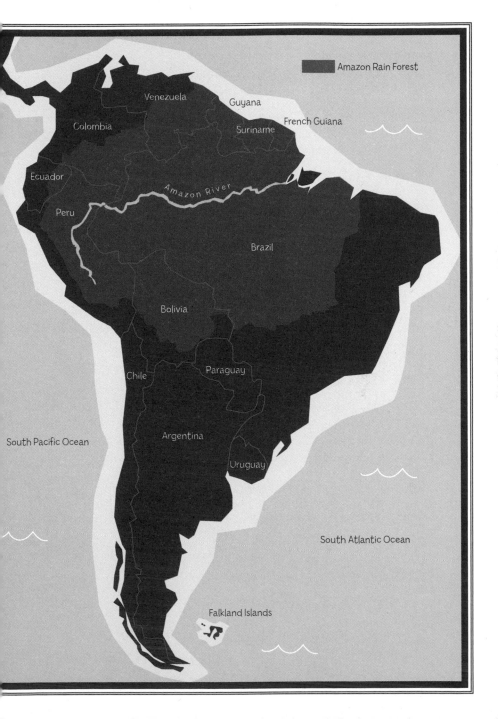

Amazon Rain Forest

Venezuela

Guyana

Colombia

Suriname

French Guiana

Ecuador

Amazon River

Peru

Brazil

Bolivia

Chile

Paraguay

South Pacific Ocean

Argentina

Uruguay

South Atlantic Ocean

Falkland Islands

SOFIA'S MACAW FACTS

The scarlet macaws were the most amazing to see! Here are my favorite macaw facts.

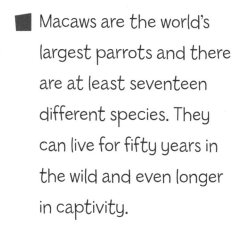

■ Macaws are the world's largest parrots and there are at least seventeen different species. They can live for fifty years in the wild and even longer in captivity.

■ Hyacinth macaws are the length of a full-size guitar. They are a rich blue color, with yellow around their eyes and beaks.

■ Military macaws are mostly bright green, as though they are wearing a soldier's uniform.

■ Blue-and-yellow macaws have golden feathers on their bellies and the underside of their wings. They are good at copying human voices!

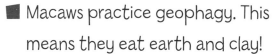

■ Macaws are loud! Their cries can be heard from miles away.

■ Macaws practice geophagy. This means they eat earth and clay!

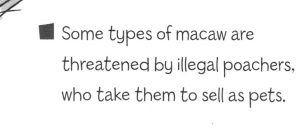

■ Some types of macaw are threatened by illegal poachers, who take them to sell as pets.

HOW CAN WE HELP SAVE THE AMAZON?

There are a few things everyone can do to help preserve the amazing habitat of the Amazon rain forest.

Be careful what your family buys—look out for labels that tell you that foods (like bananas or coffee), furniture, and toys have been made in a responsible way that doesn't harm the rain forest.

Use less energy! A lot of our electricity is produced by burning fossil fuels, which is harmful to the Amazon rain forest and to the environment.

Eat less beef. Brazil is the world's largest provider of beef, and huge parts of the rain forest are being cleared to make room for cattle farms. The less demand there is for beef, the less land will be needed for cattle.

Paper comes from trees. Use less paper, and recycle any paper waste.